Avry and Atreus
Save Christmas

A Marshmallow the Magic Cat Adventure

Written by Dr. Kimberly Brayman

Illustrated by Irina Denissova

For information regarding permission please write to

Dr. Kimberly Brayman: info@KimberlyBraymanAuthor.com

For bulk and wholesale orders please email

Dr. Kimberly Brayman: info@KimberlyBraymanAuthor.com

ISBN: 978-1-951688-06-6 (paperback)

Written by Dr. Kimberly Brayman

Illustrated by Irina Denissova

First Edition

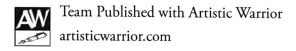
Team Published with Artistic Warrior
artisticwarrior.com

May we all keep the magic alive!

Table of Contents

Company Is Coming

It was a few days before Christmas. The slightly crooked old house perched on the mountainside shimmered with magic. Marshmallow the cat padded down its halls, a peaceful sentinel watching over the house.

As he explored the house, it creaked as if to say, "I deserve to be here as much as the trees of the forest."

The fairies in the hallway flew around Marshmallow and waved at him. This was their home too.

Marshmallow went into the bedroom where his best friend, Avry, sat on her bed with her mama.

"We have company coming, Marshmallow," Avry said as she stuck out her pointy chin. "I'm not sure I want anyone else here."

Avry's mama sighed. "Avry, our family from China is coming to visit. We need to make your cousin, Atreus, feel welcome."

Marshmallow jumped up on the bed and sat beside Avry.

Avry tried to ignore her mother's comment. "Mama, the coyotes sang to me last night. And look, the sun is waking up in the lake."

A dreamy look came into her mama's eyes. "It is lovely here, isn't it?" her mother said, as she looked out Avry's large bedroom window. The sparkling, crystal-blue-white snow in the yard was glistening, and the sun looked alive as it rose up out of the silver lake.

Marshmallow had billowing tufts of fur, green eyes, and a twisted left ear. He turned to look at Avry's mother and blinked. Then he reached over and gently batted at a Christmas tree ornament on the small tree next to Avry's bed. He loved living here.

"Avry, please. You need to get dressed," Mama said softly. "Company's coming."

Marshmallow looked away from the tree and looked right at Avry. Without words he reminded her, "We are all special, but family matters most of all."

People Matter More Than Things

Avry heard people coming in the front door of the old farmhouse. She was a sensitive girl who did not like loud noises or bright lights. She didn't like tags on her clothes or scratchy things. She didn't like waistbands on pants or short sleeves on shirts. She most certainly didn't like hurrying for people.

"Nope," she said to Marshmallow. "No company for me."

Marshmallow looked over at Avry. "You are a kind girl, Avry. And you're my magical best friend. We know what we need to do."

Avry looked at Marshmallow. She touched his new Christmas collar and wondered if the Christmas elves were wrapping presents, or if the penguins and polar bears were having a Christmas dance at the North Pole.

She sighed, leaving her thoughts behind. It was very cold outside and three days until Christmas. Avry didn't want people, even family, in her crooked farmhouse.

As Avry daydreamed about penguins and polar bears, her bedroom door burst open. Her cousin, Atreus, stood there. He was three years older than Avry and tall, really tall, much taller than Avry.

Avry was always the smallest in her class, the smallest on her soccer team, and the smallest at the store. Sometimes, when she tried to pay for something herself, the clerk would have to stand on tip-toes to peer over the counter to see her little determined face. "I am big enough," she would think. "I am smart, and I can shop by myself."

People don't need to be tall to do things. Avry knew this. Her mama knew this. Her nana knew this. Her best friend, Marshmallow, knew this. Avry wasn't sure if Atreus knew this.

Atreus was full of energy. He ran over to the bed, punched Avry on her arm, and then went over to the window and looked out.

"Are the bunnies out? Is the hoot owl still here? What else is happening in the woods today?" Avry went to the window and looked out too.

Avry hoped Atreus remembered the magic they saw last summer. She hoped that Atreus would know that even though she was small, she was important too.

She knew big kids sometimes thought little kids were unimportant or couldn't do things.

Atreus looked at Avry and smiled. When she saw his kind smile, she knew it was going to be alright.

Avry's mama pulled an old rusty cot and an old wooden screen out of the attic and set them up in Avry's room. Avry wasn't sure she wanted to share her room or her best friend, Marshmallow.

Avry and Atreus talked and Atreus told her he liked to read books and draw. Avry brought out paper and coloured pencils and they both started to draw.

After a while, Avry decided she liked having Atreus there. He drew magical pictures of Marshmallow and a brave knight.

They both looked at each other's drawings with interest just as their nana had taught them. Nana always said, "People matter more than things."

Nana also said, "Things that bring you joy should be done with gusto."

Avry thought that was such a good word. Gusto! It means you do things that you love with your whole heart, like singing.

Nana had come to her Christmas concert last week. She beamed as Avry sang every Christmas carol as loudly as she could.

When she practiced, Marshmallow blinked his green eyes, and with one eye going up and one down he told her, "Your singing sounds perfect to me."

The Raven Brings a Message

Avry remembered how Nana had taught her and Atreus about magic and how to find it. She taught them how to see the shimmer of magic on the lake in the morning, and how to feel the magic in the forest behind her house. Now it was Christmas, and the magic sparkled around them.

Avry and Atreus could both feel in their bellies that something was about to happen. They skootched up on their knees at the window ledge, looked into the distance and waited.

A raven flew out of the darkness of the woods and landed on a branch, just out of the sun, on the tall knotty tree outside of Avry's bedroom.

The raven was huge, as long as two cobs of corn, with eyes as black as the darkest night. His feathers shimmered with sapphire blue mixed with flecks of gold. They knew this raven had flown here to find them. "Caw, caw," the raven called. "Caw, caw."

Avry and Atreus turned in astonishment when they heard, "Caw, caw," beside them.

Marshmallow, the giant, magical, marmalade-colored cat, was answering the raven. With a quizzical look, they turned back to look at the raven.

Ever so quietly, underneath the *caw, caw* of the raven, they could hear the words, "Save Christmas, save Christmas." Then the raven waited.

Avry and Atreus could see a small scroll of birch bark left on the branch, tied with a red ribbon.

"How . . . how are we going to get that?" Atreus asked.

Marshmallow knew how to get the scroll. He quietly got up, padded down the hall, and climbed the attic stairs. He went to the corner of the dusty attic where one of the shingles was hinged.

Marshmallow leapt onto the tree, landed gracefully, and picked up the scroll.

Avry and Atreus cheered. Then the raven nodded and flew away.

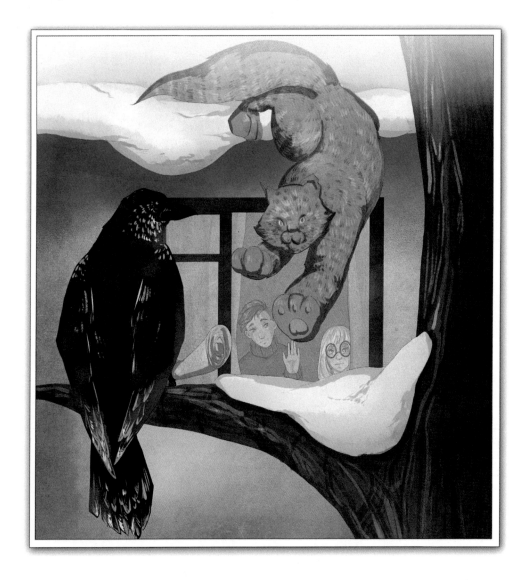

A few seconds later, Marshmallow appeared beside them with a light dusting of snow on his long, orange fur. He dropped the scroll beside them.

Avry and Atreus untied the ribbon. "Hurry and save Christmas," it said. They looked at each other. They shrugged their shoulders. They didn't know what to do.

Their nana said that sometimes not knowing was exactly the right place to be. She said that often people make up their minds too quickly, without considering all the possibilities. They knew they would have to pay attention to solve this mystery.

Gellatly Nut Farm

Later that evening, after a spaghetti dinner that Avry's mama and dad made, they all bundled up and headed to Gellatly Nut Farm.

Avry and Atreus noticed there were lots of little elves peeking out of the trees and even inside the tents. They spotted one little elf who wore a pointed, gold hat and green shoes and mittens. She was operating the hot chocolate dispenser and filling mugs of steaming hot chocolate.

Avry and Atreus realized not everyone saw the elves. If they did not believe in magic, in even the tiniest little part of them, the elf would have to jump out of the way while they tried to make the hot chocolate dispenser work. After a few tries, they got their drink.

It was quite possible the hot chocolate that came out was not the same when non-magical people poured it. Avry knew magic made everything better. When the little elf filled their mugs, the children smiled at her, and the elf laughed and laughed. Their hot chocolate was frothy, and little marshmallows popped up in their mugs. It tasted like peppermint and filled them with warmth.

The two families walked past row after row of trees covered in Christmas lights. Atreus's mama and dad marveled at the fifty thousand lights. Atreus's dad stomped his cold feet in the snow.

Avry and Atreus looked for clues to solve the Christmas mystery.

They could see dozens of Christmas elves peeking out behind ornaments and branches. Some elves were sitting on the tree branches. They were swinging their little feet with the bells, and the tinkle could be heard, if you stopped being noisy. They wondered where everyone else thought the jingle bell music was coming from.

Avry closed her eyes and could hear the soft breeze swishing the branches. Atreus could hear the gentle hoot of a hoot owl. They both heard the silvery tinkle of little elf feet making music.

Avry turned to Atreus. "How are a couple of kids supposed to save Christmas?" She sometimes wanted to give up on things when it felt too hard.

Atreus smiled and said, "My dad and I solve problems all the time. Two heads are better than one, Avry." Curiosity lit up Atreus's eyes. "If we look for the answers, we will find them."

Avry wished Marshmallow was there to help them. Then, out of the corner of her eye, where magic appears, came another giant raven. It was black and emerald green with coal-black eyes. In its mouth was a second birch scroll tied with a red ribbon.

The raven left the message high in a pine tree. Atreus's dad, who was very tall, glanced over and saw it.

"Dad, will you get that for us, please?" Atreus asked.

Avry and Atreus Save Christmas: A Marshmallow the Magic Cat Adventure

Atreus hadn't seen the little mouse that was ready to scamper up the branches.

Atreus's dad, who sometimes saw magic, said, "Just in time. I think this little wood mouse was going to get it. Here you go."

Avry giggled at the little wood mouse dressed all in holiday style. The mouse's little eyes glimmered with mischief. His top hat and tails looked ready for a holiday party. Atreus noticed the mouse was drinking a tiny mug of hot chocolate. He laughed and pointed to the mouse. Avry laughed too.

A group of carolers gathered next to Avry and Atreus. Avry couldn't resist, and she and twenty or thirty children and adults sang along to "Jingle Bells." Avry sang to the very end. She looked over at Atreus, who was waving the scroll at her.

She smiled, left the group of singers, and walked back to Atreus. He opened the scroll and they read it together. The message said, "Untie the children."

"Now what does this mean?" Avry said to Atreus.

"I have no idea," Atreus said. "Let's look for clues."

Everywhere Avry and Atreus looked there were children. They were puzzled, but Atreus knew they would persevere. They would find the children they needed to untie.

Avry felt her determination kick in. "We can do this, Atreus. The ravens and elves are helping us. We will save Christmas!"

After an hour of gazing at lights, drinking hot chocolate, and singing Christmas carols, the two families drove home to the crooked farmhouse.

As soon as Avry and Atreus's sleepy heads hit the pillow, they were fast asleep.

A hoot owl watched them from a tree outside Avry's window.

Three ravens sat in the darkness on the tree branch. The light of the moon reflected off their feathers.

They all sat and waited patiently for morning.

Stuart Park Skating Rink

Avry and Atreus woke early. They ate warm oatmeal while their parents chatted and had coffee.

When breakfast was over, they all bundled up and headed to Stuart Park, in downtown Kelowna, to skate by the lake.

Avry said, "I'm not very good at skating."

Atreus said, "I've never tried." They did not have a skating rink where he lived. While he was an excellent swimmer, he did not know how to glide along on the frozen water.

The children fell as often as they stayed on their feet. They both remembered that trying is what's important.

Atreus was very generous with his compliments, shouting, "Way to go, Avry. You're doing a great job!" Atreus, a little slower to begin, soon rushed along.

Avry shouted, "You're awesome at skating."

Just before lunchtime, Atreus saw another raven. He pointed it out to Avry. "Look, a third raven."

It walked towards them on the crusty snow at the edge of the skating rink. This raven was black with shimmering gold and silver in its feathers. It dropped a scroll into Avry's outstretched hand. "Caw, caw," the raven said. Avry and Atreus heard, "The children are acting mean."

Avry and Atreus gasped. Nothing ruins Christmas more than nasty people. Every time a child acts mean, a little bit of magic disappears.

Atreus walked back over to Avry, scroll in hand.

"The mystery is," Atreus said, "who are these mean children, and where will we find them?"

"We found the first clue in the big tree behind my window, and we found the second clue at Gellatly Nut Farm," Avry said.

Atreus nodded and said, "Yes, and now we have a third clue from the skating rink. We're running out of time, Avry. It's only two days until Christmas."

Just then, a whole group of elves appeared from behind a large tree at the side of the glassy skating rink. These elves were not the same as the ones at Gellatly Nut Farm. They were not the same as the elves at Avry's house.

These elves had dirty beards and bulbous noses. Angry scowls filled their faces. They were lazy elves who had chosen not to work at the North Pole. They'd chosen not to help make children happy at Christmas.

Avry and Atreus stared at them.

Then Atreus said, "Avry, I've heard about these elves. They made a poor choice. They've been selfish, and they get nastier over time."

The pair watched as the mean elves pulled a large group of children along, all wound in strands of broken Christmas lights.

Avry and Atreus looked around and could see bits of Christmas magic disappearing. The children were still being mean as the elves pulled them along. They were scowling and insulting each other and everyone who walked by. Avry and Atreus saw one boy trip another. They heard one girl tell another girl, "You're ugly."

Every time the rude children did something nasty, Avry and Atreus saw the shimmer in the air grow thinner. It wasn't as bright or happy here. They could see the grownups didn't look as happy as they'd been a few moments ago.

"Those mean children are going to ruin Christmas," Avry whispered to Atreus.

"I think the elves found the bullies and kids who are nasty to their brothers and sisters and brought them here. I think they were already mean, otherwise these elves wouldn't be able to capture them."

Avry and Atreus watched as the trouble-making elves encouraged the children to act even meaner.

Marshmallow to the Rescue

Avry and Atreus knew they needed to act. They knew when they worked together they could solve problems. This was Christmas they were saving.

Avry felt deep inside herself, to the magic place she knew was there. She wished, and said inside, "Marshmallow, help us."

Best friends do show up when you need them.

Out of the darkness, with a twinkle of bells, came a tiny sleigh pulled by Marshmallow. The sleigh was filled with happy elves. Marshmallow had used his magic to fly to the North Pole to pick up these good elves who worked with Santa. These elves were smiling and cheering Avry and Atreus on.

"Look, Atreus, Santa's elves." Avry pointed up to the sky. The elves were drifting down from the sleigh with little parachutes.

As Marshmallow circled, the elves went *snip, snip, snip* and cut the wires that held the children together.

"Atreus, meanness has been growing inside these children for a long time," Avry said.

"Yes, Avry," Atreus agreed, thinking back to his last visit with Nana. "And the meaner you are, the more the darkness grows."

Nana had told him, "Atreus, you will be tempted to act mean if you spend time with kids who do mean things. When there is darkness inside a child, there is less room for magic."

Avry and Atreus could see Marshmallow throwing handfuls of elf dust from the sleigh.

It landed on the mean elves and on the mean children's heads. As the wires dropped away, the children's eyes started to light up with Christmas magic.

"Help us!" the children called.

"Help us," said the grumpy elves as the magic of Christmas once more entered their hearts. "Help us save Christmas!

Avry and Atreus knew they needed to forgive the children and elves, even if it was hard to do. Nana had told them that everyone makes mistakes.

"Everyone is tempted to be mean sometimes," Atreus said to Avry.

"We all feel grumpy sometimes," Avry said.

"We're coming!" Avry and Atreus ran over to the once-mean children and elves.

Avry and Atreus looked at each other and took each other's hands. Atreus turned and said to the children, "Hold hands."

A small child nodded his head and said to the mean elves, "Take our hands."

Avry and Atreus looked up and nodded to Marshmallow. "Marshmallow," Avry said, "we're saving Christmas!"

In the blink of an eye, Avry and Atreus forgave the children and elves for being mean and saying mean things.

The blink of an eye is exactly how long magic takes.

Avry and Atreus knew these children and elves would need help after Christmas to stay nice.

They heard Marshmallow speaking in their minds. "They will all need our help to stay kind. Kindness grows faster than meanness. If we are kind, thoughtful, and forgiving all year long, we can save every Christmas."

Santa's Arrival

Avry and Atreus heard a "Ho! Ho! Ho!" and watched as Santa appeared. He was surrounded by billowing clouds of magic elf dust. With him were the three ravens, now in holiday hats with bells on. Little elves sat on the cozy rim of Santa's hat. There were jingle bells on the top of Santa's big, black boots.

Marshmallow jumped onto Santa's left shoulder and playfully reached around Santa's red hat and big, silver beard to bat at the ravens. They cawed and flew away.

Santa laughed and put Marshmallow on the ice beside Avry and Atreus.

Santa looked at the once-mean elves. They were smiling. "You may all join me at the North Pole," Santa said. "There's still more work to be done before Christmas."

All the elves cheered together. "We want to help! We want to help!"

Santa smiled and turned to Marshmallow, Avry, and Atreus. He said, "By being curious and kind, and by working together and forgiving others, you have all saved Christmas."

Avry and Atreus's eyes were as big as saucers.

Then Avry found her voice. "Thank you, Santa. I love you, Marshmallow. I love you, Atreus. And we all love Christmas!"

And just like that, in the blink of an eye, which is exactly how long magic takes, Santa and his sleigh were gone.

Discussion Questions & Activities

1. Avry doesn't like it when she gets company. Do you like getting company? _____

    _____

    _____

    _____

2. Avry is sensitive and doesn't like loud noises or scratchy tags on her clothes. What don't you like? _____

    _____

    _____

    _____

3. Avry has to share her room with Atreus over the holidays. Do you ever have to share your room? _____
    How does that make you feel? _____

    _____

    _____

    _____

    _____

    _____

    _____

4. Gellatly Nut Farm is a real nut farm in a regional park in West Kelowna, British Columbia. Stuart Park and its outdoor skating rink are also real places in Kelowna, British Columbia. Do you have a special place you like to visit at Christmas time? _____

   _____

   _____

   _____

5. Ask your parents or adult caregivers if they had any special traditions at Christmas when they were little. Can you do them now, or do you do them already? _____

   _____

   _____

   _____

6. Are you tempted to be mean sometimes? When? _____

   _____

   _____

   How can you help yourself to make a better choice?

   _____

   _____

   _____

7. Why do you think some children act mean? _____

_____

_____

_____

Do you think it is something inside them, a bad habit, or a choice they make? _____

_____

_____

_____

8. Atreus enjoys solving the Christmas mystery. Avry starts out frustrated. How do you feel when you are trying to solve something?_____

_____

_____

_____

9. What is your biggest problem or issue you would like to solve? _____

_____

_____

_____

10. Avry and Atreus are on a mission to save Christmas. It is very important to them. Why? _____

_____

_____

_____

11. Marshmallow is Avry's best friend. She does not want to share him. Do you have a best friend that you do not like to share? Who? _____

_____

_____

Do you have any suggestions that might help Avry? ____

_____

_____

_____

_____

_____

12. The ravens help solve the Christmas mystery by bringing the scrolls. Who do you think wrote the scrolls? _____

_____

_____

_____

13. Do you believe that being kind to someone can fill you with happiness? _____

_____

_____

14. Find a way to be extra kind to someone without telling them why. Write how you feel here. _____

_____

_____

_____

_____

_____

15. What do you like the most about Christmas? _____

_____

_____

_____

_____

_____

_____

_____

_____

About the Author

Dr. Kimberly Brayman is a licensed psychologist who resides in British Columbia, Canada.

After decades of working in health care, she is inspired to build confidence, normalize struggle, encourage hope, and delight adults and children alike through her storytelling.

She believes stories build empathy and empower the listener to find their own self-reliance and strength.

The power of supportive relationships is a theme that runs through all her books.

When a child knows deep in their heart that they are loved and accepted, just the way they are, they have a chance to blossom and thrive.

In this series, Avry is a highly-sensitive, anxious girl who develops capability and courage and gains insight with every adventure.

Her magic cat, Marshmallow, is her best friend and near-constant companion. They are joined by friends, family members, elves, fairies, animals, and magic in this series.

Dr. Kimberly Brayman is a registered psychologist (registration #2464) in British Columbia, Canada and, until 2020, was a registered psychologist in Colorado, USA.

About the Illustrator

Irina Denissova loves creating illustrations for children's books. Her creative talents bring a magical atmosphere to stories, making them enjoyable for both parents and children. She believes the best part about being an illustrator is that she helps create a new world for readers.

She lives in Temirtau, Kazakhstan and, in her spare time, loves to read and create whatever drawings pop into her mind.

The author describes her as a humble, unbelievably talented young woman who has a near-magical ability to take descriptions and characters and create what the author sees in her own mind.

Books by Dr. Kimberly Brayman

Other Marshmallow the Magic Cat Adventures

Avry's Magical Cat: A Marshmallow the Magic Cat Adventure
Avry adopts a magical cat from the animal shelter. Avry has a magical view of the world, and every day she learns the value of good friends, love and family.

A Troll in the Woods: A Marshmallow the Magic Cat Adventure
A true quest that shows courage and fear can go hand in hand, and the power of friendship can inspire action. Available on Amazon now.

Marshmallow Paints the Town: A Marshmallow the Magic Cat Adventure
A fun story that focuses on collaboration, self-responsibility, making mistakes, and recovering.

A Trip to the Hot Springs: A Marshmallow the Magic Cat Adventure
A lovely story with a focus on friendship, magic, and skills to assist with anxiety.

Illustrated Children's Books

Nana Loves You More

Artsy Alphabet

Count With Me

I Want to Be

Blueberries

I Am Different and I Am the Same

Check the author's website at KimberlyBraymanAuthor.com for updates.

Books can be purchased directly from Amazon. For larger orders, please contact the author for wholesale pricing.

Marshmallow the Magic Cat Adventure Books.

Available now on Amazon.

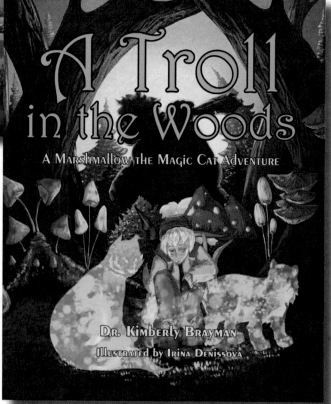

I Want To Be, is a rhyming book for children ages 0-4. Kids love this fun, easy-to-read storybook. The magical ideas will delight your child. It is sure to become a favorite. Available now on Amazon.

Avry and Atreus Save Christmas: A Marshmallow the Magic Cat Adventure

Made in the USA
Las Vegas, NV
11 December 2021

37167549R00038